Lionel and Amelia

This edition first published in the United States of America in 1996 by
MONDO Publishing
By arrangement with MULTIMEDIA INTERNATIONAL (UK) LTD

For information contact:
MONDO Publishing
One Plaza Road
Greenvale, New York 11548

Printed in Singapore
First Mondo printing, July 1996
96 97 98 99 00 01   9 8 7 6 5 4 3 2 1

Originally published in Australia in 1988 by Horwitz Publications Pty Ltd
Original development by Robert Andersen & Associates and Snowball Educational
Cover redesign by David Neuhaus/NeuStudio

Library of Congress Cataloging-in-Publication Data

Peguero, Leone.
Lionel and Amelia / by Leone Peguero ; illustrated by Adrian Peguero and Gerard Peguero.
p. cm.
"Originally published in Australia in 1988 by Horwitz Publications Pty. Ltd."
Summary: A tale of two mouse children, Lionel and Amelia, one very neat and the other very messy, who become friends.
ISBN 1-57255-197-6 (pbk. : alk. paper)
[1. Mice—Fiction. 2. Orderliness—Fiction 3. Friendship—Fiction.]
I. Peguero, Adrian, ill. II. Peguero, Gerard, 1950- ill. III. Title.
PZ7.P35835Li 1996
[Fic]—dc20
95-49117
CIP
AC

by Leone Peguero

Illustrated by Adrian Peguero and Gerard Peguero

Lionel Mouse was the oldest of three mouse children. He lived with his family in a cozy mouse hole where he was lucky enough to have his very own room.

Being a tidy sort of mouse, Lionel remembered to brush his teeth after every meal and to comb his fur carefully each morning when he dressed. He always put his toys away in their special places and hung up his clothes.

But keeping everything spic-and-span was not always easy for Lionel, with a younger brother, a baby sister, and several cousins who loved nothing better than to explore his oh-so-tidy bedroom.

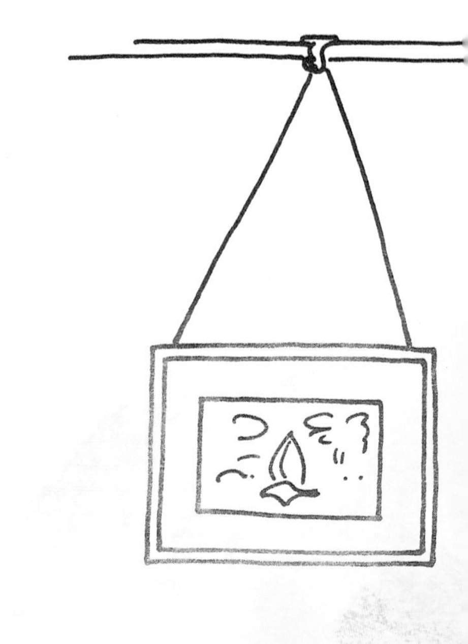

Nearby there lived another mouse named Amelia. She also had her own little room. It was at the top of her family's large, rambling mouse hole.

Amelia and her family loved bright, warm colors, unusual pets, and loud, cheery music. Amelia didn't mind a bit if her room was quite messy.

One day Amelia came to Lionel's mouse hole to play with one of his cousins. Amelia and Lionel had never met before, but once they had, somehow things were never quite the same again.

They found playing together fun, especially skateboarding.

When they took a break, Lionel and Amelia discovered they both loved crispy cheese puffs, twirly ice creams, and whizzo drinks best of all.

They shared everything happily.

Before Amelia went home, Lionel put his skateboard tidily in his room.

When Amelia saw his room she stared in amazement at the cool order and tidiness of it all. Nothing was crushed or crumpled, broken or out of place.

"Why, it's so . . . NEAT!" she gasped, taking a new look at Lionel.

"Not so you'd notice," insisted Lionel, who couldn't imagine how else a bedroom might look.

THE RATTY HORROR SHOW
Great mouse-traps!

The next day Lionel visited Amelia and saw her family's mouse hole and Amelia's little attic room. This time it was his turn to be amazed. Such color, sound, and confusion!

Some time later Lionel's family was shocked when he arrived at the breakfast table looking like a very different mouse.

Being friends with Amelia had certainly made a difference in Lionel.

His fur was no longer neatly brushed down and his clothes had frayed edges. His shirt was covered with iron-on crayon writing, which his parents could see at once would not come off, even in the whitest of white washes.

Next Lionel's family discovered that his
bedroom had also changed a great deal.

Instead of being another neat and tidy room in their cozy little mouse hole, Lionel's room was now like a red hot pepper in a bag of cucumbers.

Lionel's family was shocked, and his little brother and sister were now rather frightened of him. Could this noisy, colorful mouse really be their once quiet, tidy brother?

His worried mother and father drank many cups of tea and talked well into the night. They discussed just where they had gone wrong in the tricky business of mouse-raising.

Meanwhile, Amelia was also trying out a new image for herself and her mouse hole bedroom.

Out went the bright and colorful and in came the cool and neat. What a shock for her family as well!

Amelia's family didn't mind so much about the changes she made to herself and her own room.

But they certainly did object when they realized
she had plans to reorganize the entire mouse hole.

Lionel and Amelia still played together, but things weren't quite the same as before.

Amelia had to peer very hard at Lionel to make sure it really was him. In his new clothes, he looked just like everyone in her family and their friends.

Lionel had much the same trouble. When they played tag, he kept mistaking Amelia for one of his many cousins.

There was no longer that special difference from most of their families and friends they both had enjoyed so much.

Playing together wasn't as much fun anymore.

But good friends can always find a way around their problems. Lionel decided to be the neat little mouse he'd always been, which secretly he found much easier.

And Amelia decided to be just herself again.

Although it should be admitted that neither of them

was ever quite the same again.